Maribel's Year

Written by
Michelle Sterling

Illustrated by
Sarah Gonzales

KATHERINE TEGEN BOOKS
An Imprint of HarperCollins Publishers

JANUARY

First steps,
first snow.
New country,
new home.

I miss the swish of fresh carabao milk
on our doorstep every morning.
And friends and family
dropping in for merienda
and chats in our courtyard.

Here it's quiet steps.
Quiet everything.

FEBRUARY

I learned some English in the Philippines,
but the English here is a foggy soup of strange words.
Their spelling makes no sense!
I almost forget the last e in *valentine*
because it's silent.

My first valentine—
a handful of sour candy
with a sweet message
from my first friend.
I hope she'll be my best friend.

I paint a ruby heart to send
with my last chocolate peppermint
on an eight-thousand-mile journey
to Papa in Makati.
I tell him how much
I miss feeding the koi in our pond
with him every morning.

MARCH

Gray shivers
and rain
and my boots stuck in
the mud.

But in our mailbox,
a package peeks out
with my name in neat, exact writing
. . . from Papa!

Wrapped in banana leaves
is a painting of our trip to
Batan Island last year,
where we camped and stargazed and swam
in a sea of constellations.

APRIL

Drops of sun on my face,
buds and pear blossoms,
tangles of ivy,
and growing green.

To celebrate Papa's birthday,
we make his favorite—pinakbet.
And for a second I almost hear
Papa in our kitchen cooking it:
the clay pot shaken
twice, and quickly,
just like he does,
with a spoonful of shrimp paste on top.

MAY

Wobbly knees,
whirring wheels,
wind in my hair,
down the hill
on my first bike ride ever!

I write Papa a letter about it
the minute I get home
and send him a map I drew
from the Philippines to us.
X marks our house on the hill
so he knows the way.

JUNE

Avocado shakes in the blender hum
it's summer, it's summer!

Toes peek out of my new red sandals,
wet, moppy hair,
fish, chips, and sea-salt air.
Saltwater taffy as salty as the sea,
and orange sherbet like a dream,
which Papa would love.

Sunlight stretches
into long afternoons.
Mama calls me in for dinner
through the window,
but I stay out a minute more to watch
the moonflowers open.

Another package has arrived.
Through the crinkly yellow paper
a sweet smell tickles my nose . . .
slivers of my favorite dried mango
and tamarind from Lolo's farm in Pangasinan!
Papa's letter says to be patient.
He promises to join us as soon as he can.

JULY

Hot sun
and swinging buckets
for strawberry hunting.
The ripest and reddest
I've ever seen.
One pocketful for now
and one pocketful for later.

The hot days here remind me of summer in Bulacan
listening to Papa's old bossa nova records
and drinking buko juice
in the cool of our bamboo garden.

AUGUST

Tiny pink clouds
and purple skies.
A secret meeting
at the walnut tree
for a strange and magical light show.

I put my glowing jar
next to Papa's constellation map
and dream of a time when I'll take him here.

SEPTEMBER

Now is when the holiday season starts
in the Philippines.
Red, green, and yellow
are the huge parols Papa makes by hand
to hang up on the doors
of all my titos and titas' homes.

Monsoon season is still soaking the country.
I used to hear it all come down on the roof
while helping Papa in his workshop.

But here, summer is taking one last warm breath
as Mama sets my alarm clock for an early morning rise.

School again.
New rules
and some new faces.
(I'm thankful for a familiar one!)

OCTOBER

Pumpkin mush between my fingers,
pumpkin seeds between my teeth.
Apples up to our knees
and the air feels like
electricity.

Ringing doorbells,
dodging dinosaurs and princesses,
I look up for a moment and see
a falling star.
I close my eyes and make a wish on it—
is one star enough
to make a wish come true?

NOVEMBER

Windy orange sunsets,
shorter days, cozier nights.
Turkey, gravy, and ube pie
for our first Thanksgiving.

Mama steeps ginger in hot water
stirred with squeezes of kalamansi and honey
to make us salabat tea
as we read Papa's latest letter.

DECEMBER

Cold cheeks,
crisp noses,
a blue-black night,
and we are standing under the stars
that Papa's plane is following.

One last star leads Papa to us.
Our first Christmas back together—
all together!

In this snowy, quiet place
that finally feels like . . .

home.

For my parents and their own journey across oceans.
—M.S.

For my mom and dad, my foundation and inspiration.
—S.G.

Katherine Tegen Books is an imprint of HarperCollins Publishers.

Maribel's Year
Text copyright © 2023 by Michelle Sterling
Illustrations copyright © 2023 by Sarah Gonzales
All rights reserved. Manufactured in Italy.

Library of Congress Control Number: 2022938130
ISBN 978-0-06-311435-7

The artist used pencil on paper colored digitally to create the illustrations for this book.
Designed by Dana Fritts
Handlettering by Kristle Marshall
23 24 25 26 27 RTLO 10 9 8 7 6 5 4 3 2 1
❖
First Edition